# THE FOX
# AND THE HARE

**Retold by**
## Mirra Ginsburg

**Illustrated by**
## Victor Nolden

CROWN PUBLISHERS, INC. NEW YORK

Printed in the United States of America
Library of Congress Catalog Card Number: 75–90993
Published simultaneously in Canada by
General Publishing Company Limited

There were once two neighbors, a Fox and a Hare. The Fox lived in a house made of ice. The Hare lived in a house made of wood.

All winter the Fox teased the Hare:

"My house is bright, your house is dark!

My house is bright, your house is dark!"

1521615

Spring came, and the sun rose high, and the Fox's house
melted away. But the Hare's house was still as good as new.

The Fox had no place to sleep. He came to the Hare
and begged:

"Please let me in for the night."

But the Hare said:

"No. You laughed at me all winter. I won't let you in."

The Fox asked once, and the Fox asked twice, and the third time the Hare took pity on him. He opened the door, and the Fox came in. And as soon as he was in, he took the broom and chased the Hare out.

The Hare walked down the road, crying bitterly. Then he met a Dog.

"Woof, woof! Why are you crying?"

And the Hare said:

"How can I help crying? I had a wood house, and the Fox had an ice house. He asked me to let him in, and he chased me out."

"Don't cry, little Hare! I will help you."

They came to the house and the Dog barked:
"Woof, woof! Who is under that roof?
Bow, wow! Get out now!"

But the Fox replied from his nice cozy bed:
"I'll come out, I'll jump out!
  I will scratch your eyes out!"
The Dog got frightened and ran away.

Again the Hare walked down the road, crying. Then he met a Bear.

"Why are you crying, little Hare?"

"How can I help crying? I had a wood house, and the Fox had an ice house. He asked me to let him in, and he chased me out."

"Don't cry, I will help you!"

"No, you won't! The Dog could not help me, and neither will you."

"Oh, yes, I will, just watch me!"

They came to the house, and the Bear growled:
"Ho-ho-ho!
    You'd better go!"

But the Fox replied from his window:
"I'll come out, I'll jump out,
 I will scratch your eyes out!"
The Bear got frightened and ran away.

The Hare walked down the road again, till he met a Bull.

"Why are you crying, little Hare?"

"How can I help crying? I had a wood house, and the Fox had an ice house. He asked me to let him in, and he chased me out."

"Come, I will help you!"

"No, you won't! The Dog could not help me, and the Bear could not help me, and neither will you."

"Oh, yes, I will, just watch me!"

They came to the house, and the Bull bellowed:

"Moo-whoo!

Out with you!"

But the Fox replied from his nice cozy bed:
"I'll come out, I'll jump out,
    I will scratch your eyes out!"
The Bull got frightened and ran away.

The Hare walked down the road again, till he met a Rooster.

"Cock-a-doodle-doo! What's the matter with you? Why are you crying?"

"How can I help crying? I had a wood house, and the Fox had an ice house. He asked me to let him in, and he chased me out."

"Is that all? Come, I will help you."

"No, you won't! The Dog could not help me, and the Bear could not help me, and the Bull could not help me, and neither will you."

"Oh, yes, I will. Just come and see!"

They came to the house, and the Rooster made a great, big noise. He stamped his feet, and he flapped his wings, and he pecked at the window:

"I'll crow and I'll shout
Cock-a-doodle-doo! 1521615
If you don't get out,
I'll come after you!"
The Fox got frightened and cried:
"Just let me put my shoes on!"

The Rooster stamped his feet a second time, and he flapped his wings, and he pecked at the window:
"I'll crow and I'll shout
Cock-a-doodle-doo!
If you don't get out,
I'll come after you!
I have sharp black spurs,
Look out for your furs!"
And the Fox begged:
"Just let me get dressed!"

The Rooster stamped his feet a third time, and he flapped
his wings, and he pecked at the window:
"I'll crow and I'll shout
Cock-a-doodle-doo!
If you don't get out,
I'll come after you!
I have sharp black spurs,
Look out for your furs!
Ko-ko-ko,
Out you go!
Now!"

"I'm going, I'm going," cried the Fox. And he ran out of the house, and slunk through the grass, and into the bushes, and across the field, and off and away to the far, far woods. And he ran so fast that all you could see was his red tail flashing.

And the Hare and the Rooster went to live in the house
made of wood.

If you come out into the field, and go past the fence, and cross the brook, and climb up the hill, you will see their little house. They may be there still.